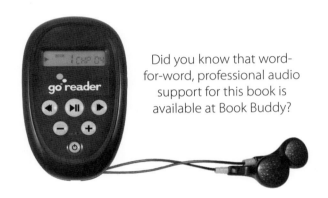

Did you know that word-for-word, professional audio support for this book is available at Book Buddy?

GoReader™ powered by Book Buddy is pre-loaded with word-for-word audio support to build strong readers and achieve Common Core standards.

The corresponding GoReader™ for this book can be found at: http://bookbuddyaudio.com

Or send an email to: info@bookbuddyaudio.com

TALES OF
THE UNCOOL

The
Misadventures
of Damien Seeley

BY KIRSTEN RUE
ILLUSTRATED BY SARA RADKA

The Misadventures of Damien Seeley
Tales of the Uncool

Scobre Educational
2255 Calle Clara
La Jolla, CA 92037

Scobre Operations & Administration
42982 Osgood Road
Fremont, CA 94539

www.scobre.com
info@scobre.com

Scobre Educational publications may be purchased for
educational, business, or sales promotional use.

Cover and layout design by Jana Ramsay
Copyedited by Renae Reed

ISBN: 978-1-62920-137-5 (Soft Cover)
ISBN: 978-1-62920-136-8 (Library Bound)
ISBN: 978-1-62920-135-1 (eBook)

Table of Contents

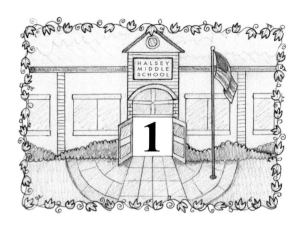

Adventure, Interrupted

Globorz Galaxy. Far, far in the past.

Saramus Dent crouched beneath a glowing boulder as the blue light from blasto-guns streamed around him.

It was the eighth year of war with the Blue Forces and the dreaded Hildebeast. He knew the Hildebeast was out there. He could hear its disgusting growl and the scratch of its footsteps.

Peaking around the corner, Dent smelled the unmistakable scent of tuna fish. The Hildebeast had found him! Springing up from his crouch, he fired his green blasto-gun. . . .

"DAMIEN. DAMIEN! GEEZ, CAN'T YOU HEAR ME?! I'VE BEEN shouting your name for like the last 10 minutes! Did you want lunch or not?"

The Hildebeast leaped up and dodged his blasto-gun blast. On its teeth, sickening metal gleamed. . . .

"Damien, I swear, if you're making me into a gross creature in your story again, I am going to tell Mom!"

"Take that, you putrescent beast!" Saramus Dent

cried as he jumped on the Hildebeast's back. It would be a fight to the death, but Dent could handle it. Bravery had always come naturally to him. . . .

"*Mo*-om! Damien's putting me in his story again! *Mooooommm!*"

"Damien, stop bothering your sister and come down and eat your sandwich!"

And with that, another chapter in the life of Saramus Dent comes to a close. I feel like it's kind of unfair that just when he's about to do something very cool, *someone* has to grind everything to a halt. And all for a gross tuna fish sandwich on wheat bread! No pickles. No flavor. As I walk down the stairs, I can still see the planet of Globorz Galaxy lit up in my head. Sometimes, it seems more real than this plain old boring house on this plain old boring street. Except, of course, Globorz Galaxy and Saramus Dent are only things I made up . . . but, just to be safe, I check behind me to be sure that the *Whiz!* of a blasto-gun beam isn't headed my way.

In the kitchen, my older sister Hildy sits at a counter

stool, eating her tuna fish sandwich and glaring at me with a blasto-gun stare of her own.

"I know you've been calling me a 'Hildebeast' in your notebook or whatever," she says. "You are SO immature. Plus, you wrote putres—or putrectelant or something. That's just mean."

"Putrescent," I correct her, feeling pretty pleased with myself. "It means a really gross rotting smell." I can't help but laugh, just a little, when I see Hildy's eyebrows scrunch into a deep frown. "And, hey! Don't look in my notebook!"

"Ugh. Whatever," she sniffs. "Damien thinks he's soooo smart because he can use the online dictionary! I bet you write all kinds of *secrets* in there, too." I hold my notebook just a little bit closer to my rib cage.

"Damien," Mom says as she comes into the room, wiping her hands on a towel, "don't you see how your words could be hurtful to Hildy?"

The truth is, I don't. How could made-up words in a made-up world hurt anyone's feelings? It's just somewhere I go to escape. I remember when I first told my dad that I wanted to be a writer, and he told me to "write what you know."

I thought that was just about the stupidest advice ever, because c'mon, who would want to read about a skinny-armed sixth grader who can barely speak up in class? For now, I would much rather spend my time in the world of Saramus Dent. Of course, "real" life always seems to have other plans. . . .

The Wilds of the Cafeteria

Saramus Dent had just returned to the all-too-familiar planet of Cafetariana. He had to admit, he didn't want to be there or speak to any of the other Green Forces.

"I don't think I'm actually from this planet," he thought to himself as he stepped out of his Litecraft. When he saw the other hunchbacked Green Forces with their frog-like legs and bulging red eyes, he thought, "Yep. I'm DEFINITELY not from here."

Lunchtime is basically the worst thing about Halsey School. I've been here since fifth grade, so I've kinda gotten used to the drill.

One, go through the most *putrescent* lunch line ever.

Two, look around at all the tables, filled with friends talking or looking at their phones.

Three, see the table with the Doomsday Geeks. Think, *Man, I don't want to sit with them again.*

Four, heave a sigh and go sit with the Doomsday Geeks anyway. They're usually talking in some kind of code that sounds like a mix between *Star Wars* and *The Matrix*. Don't get me wrong, those are two of my favorite movies, but sometimes you don't want to talk in secret code.

Today is no different. Over the sound of their "digital language," I can hear the squeals of the Sweets. They're the most popular and feared girls in school. I don't turn around—I can tell from the pitch of those squeals that they're laughing at someone. *Well, at least it's not me.*

Samantha Cho is pretty much the only person at the

table who sometimes speaks like a real-live human. Today, she's completely lost in her calculator screen. I watch her punch a long string of numbers into the keys. It's like she's making a sentence out of numbers. I wait for a moment, hoping she'll look up and notice me—maybe even smile. No luck.

Instead, I pull out my notebook, which is what I do when I don't know what *else* to do. It has a smooth leather cover with my initials, D.O.S., burned into the corner. My dad gave it to me last year. Every time I open it, it makes me feel calmer. Its soft leather smell creates a quiet, peaceful world where no loud people interrupt you. In that world, if you want to get noticed, you don't have to score the winning goal in the game or think of the perfect thing to say. You just have to exist.

The sound of the lunchroom is like an orchestra, I start writing in my notebook. The sound of S.C. tapping keys on her calculator is the drums—no, wait, the percussion. The Sweets and their ringleader, Stella, screech like really annoying violins. S.C. keeps playing her calculator song. Her hair is so shiny. Her eyelashes—

Just then, my neck starts to prickle, like it does when someone's looking at me. I put my hand over what I've been writing and look over my right shoulder.

It's Samantha Cho. She's not playing with her calculator anymore. She's leaning over the back of my chair and reading every . . . last . . . word. . . .

"Hey!" I squeak, snapping the notebook closed. I feel my whole face turn red. It starts in my chest and moves up through my neck, into my cheeks. My face feels like it's being toasted over a fire.

Samantha doesn't say anything. In fact, she looks almost as embarrassed as I am, even if she doesn't have the crazy Fire Blush to give her away. My blushes are a special thing about me. Well, special or horrible. Hildy calls them my Fire Blushes, and the name kind of stuck.

"Nice writing," Samantha says, with a shrug. She has a way of doing that—shrugging so that it seems like she's already moved on from what she's saying.

"Saramus Dent. Is that, like, a made-up guy?" she asks.

"Yeah," I say, relieved that she wasn't reading the more humiliating side of the page. "He's from a book I'm writing. About space."

"Cool," she says, shrugging again.

And with that, the end-of-lunch bell rings. The Fire Blush, however, doesn't go away.

A Certain Person

D ent hadn't seen the Hildebeast for awhile, but he knew it was only a matter of time before the beast returned. . . .

I'M SITTING AT THE KITCHEN TABLE, PUTTING OFF MY ALGEBRA homework, when I feel something wet slide down behind my ear. Hildy bursts out laughing from across the room. She's been squirting water at me from a straw. I roll my eyes. *I'm the younger "immature" brother*?! *Me*?!

"I know something," she sings in a little song.

"Good for you," I say, looking back at my notebook.

"Damien." (I ignore her.)

"Damien." (Still ignoring.)

"Damien."

"What?!" It's hard to ignore Hildy when she really wants you to pay attention. I think there must be some secret sibling class called "Annoying Your Brother in Three Easy Steps." Step Two usually involves repeating my name until I can't stand it anymore.

She grins widely. "A certain *person* told me that another *certain person* was talking about you. On the bus." Hildy and I don't usually ride the bus, so I have no clue who these "*certain people*" might be. "This *certain person* knows how you feel about another *certain person.*"

"Seriously, Hildy," I say, "You're not even making sense. I don't care about these *certain people* or whoever they are!" Despite saying this, though, I feel just a tiny blush begin to bloom under my chin. *I mean, she couldn't be talking about Samantha. . . . After she was standing over me at lunch? But how could someone else have found out? Hildy's just trying to make me crazy.* My thoughts are unraveling like the threads of a scarf.

In my notebook, I realize I've written "Samantha Cho" without meaning to. I don't think Hildy can see, but still, I close the notebook and hold it to my chest.

"You can act cool, Damien," Hildy says, "but you can't hide from me. Not even in that little notebook." She does a mean impression of me, her curly hair bouncing the more she gets into it. She's pretending to hold a notebook of her own, crossing her eyes and putting her nose close to the paper. "I'm Damien," she says, pushing her teeth out over her bottom lip. "I never talk to anyone and I just scribble in here all day. Writing *nothing!*"

"Whatever," I say. Still, a small part of my brain can't help but wonder . . . *Do I really act like that?* When I'm bent over and adding another chapter to the story of Saramus Dent, do I seem like a little mouse creature?

"A *certain person* tells me that you're an idiot," I retort. I thought that was a pretty good comeback.

Hildy just rolls her eyes.

Back in my room, I open the notebook to begin again, but all my words look dumb now. On every page, Saramus Dent is winning some battle or making everyone laugh with the perfect joke. In real life, my own sister flicks water at me and I appear like some weirdo creature from another planet—but *not* the cool kind. Suddenly, everything I thought was special about the notebook just seems like I'm fooling myself. Plus, "Samantha Cho" written there by accident on the last page makes me blush all over again. What does Samantha really think about me? Did she know that I was writing about her at lunch after all?

It's time to take a break. I stuff the notebook back into my backpack and groan. *How many more days until the end of sixth grade?*

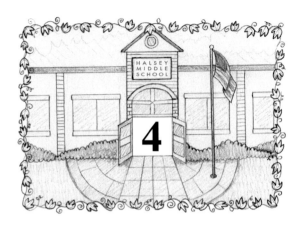

Theft!

Saramus Dent could not be found. The Green Forces looked everywhere: under the radioactive blue boulders and in every Litecraft at the dock. Without him there, they didn't really have anything to do. They couldn't really even talk. Just stand there, awkwardly, waiting for the Blue Forces to come and get them. It was kind of . . . boring. And dangerous.

Seriously, where was Saramus?!

They had no idea.

THE NEXT DAY AT SCHOOL, MY BACKPACK SLUMPS IN FRONT of my locker as I reach inside it to get my algebra book. All morning, my skin has prickled with sweat. My heart jumps in my throat every time someone looks at me or I get called on in class. Every second feels like I'm about to start running a race or take a hard test. The reason? I'm afraid of running into Samantha Cho. Overnight, my slight worry has become a full-on panic.

Earlier that morning as I crossed the walkway towards the front doors, I saw her. Samantha Cho. She was walking right in front of me. I would recognize the swish of her black hair anywhere. Not to mention her backpack covered with stickers and pins with math symbols on them. *Gulp.* Hildy's words from the day before kept echoing in my head. "A *certain someone* knows how you feel." I didn't just freeze in place. I made a sharp turn to the left and hid behind one of the big potted trees that stands next to the Halsey School doors. I pretended to look at my phone. As I hid there, I blinked and felt the points of the tree's sharp leaves digging into my cheek. I imagined Saramus Dent watching this scene and shaking his head. Dude. This is not cool.

I've known Samantha ever since third grade. The first time she spoke to me was during Mrs. Zerluski's class. She leaned over and whispered the answer to a long division problem I had been staring at. She must have noticed that my Blink Until You Get It approach was not working. (Let's just say math and I are not friends.) I showed her a little cartoon I had been drawing with captions telling the story. She smiled.

From then on, we sometimes sat together at lunch. We had been kinda sorta friends for years until two things happened:

One, suddenly, I became *so* aware that she was a GIRL (and a really kinda cute girl).

Two, for reasons I still can't understand, she started sitting with the Doomsday Geeks. Even if I could work up the courage to talk to her like the old days, I usually just get talked over or called a "noob." I mean, I always thought I was good with words, but what's a noob?!

Now I'm pretty sure I'll *never* be able to talk to her. After math class comes lunch, and there's no way I can sit at her table. I'll just have to sit in the hallway or something like that. Plus, what if other kids find out? I can't imagine the other Doomsday Geeks have even registered that a female human person has been sitting at their table for months now. . . . If Stella Sweet finds out, though, I'm done for. Even though I barely know her, she'll spread that rumor all through the sixth grade. The Human Gossip Traps, I call the Sweets in my notebook. With a sigh, I fumble for that very same notebook in my locker, except it isn't there. I check my bag. Not there either. I check my locker and bag again. And then a third time. I even check my pockets, despite knowing that they are way too small to hold a notebook.

My heart sinks to the bottom of my stomach. My face feels like someone has blasted it full-on with a blasto-gun—prickles of sweat break out across my cheeks.

The notebook is gone.

My *Adventures of Saramus Dent* and every random

thought of my days and every doodle and every time I drew a scribble of darkly-penciled fangs around the name "Stella Sweet" or wrote the words Samantha Cho . . . every note and complaint and story for a whole year . . .

All gone.

Panic

This is dangerous, Dent thought. Very dangerous. He had no way of knowing who was friend or foe. Somehow, he'd lost the Green Forces. He felt like he had a headache, like he couldn't see straight. Lights were blinking and everything was silent. Where was he? Had he somehow ended up outside of Globorz Galaxy?

"DAMIEN, OVER HERE!" I SNAP MY HEAD AROUND, HEART racing. It's Glenn, one of the Doomsday Geek kids. He waves at me. "You going to sit here?" he asks.

"Uh . . ." My eyes flash wildly back and forth. I study every face in the lunchroom, especially anyone who looks at me first. Is that girl leaning down to pick up a book she dropped? Did she drop it on purpose? Maybe she's using it as a way to lean down and whisper something to the boy sitting next to her. Or what about the Sweets? They're giggling. Typical. But aren't they looking straight at me as they do it? Even Ms. Arple, the lunch monitor, seems to be watching me closely.

It's clear someone has found my notebook, and everyone knows exactly what's in it. I'm certain of it.

My plan is to sneak some food onto my tray and escape, but I can see that's not going to happen. Glenn saying my name means that the whole Doomsday crew is now looking at me. Their eyes blink calmly at me behind their glasses. Samantha, who at first seemed to be lost in a sheet of homework, looks up.

"Did you lose something?" she asks me. Her face is completely smooth and unreadable. "I saw you at your locker and you looked really worried."

"Oh, no . . . just homework. Lots of homework. Speaking of homework, um, I have, um, some of that . . . work . . . to do. Big work." I reply. They all nod. They get work. They're always doing work. But, *big work*? I think I just won the gold medal for awkward.

"Okay," Glenn says. "I was just going to see if you wanted part of my sandwich. If you were going to sit here, I mean. Hey, also, nice job on that English poem last week! I liked how it was set in space. Pretty cool."

Samantha looks interested. "Can I read it?" she asks.

"It's . . . I don't have it with me," I reply. Because, of course, I'd stuffed it in my missing notebook.

"Oh, too bad." There's something in her face. If the other Geeks weren't sitting there and if Samantha wouldn't notice, I could take a moment to study her expression. She seems . . . suspicious.

What is going on?! The Doomsday Geeks never talk to me. Glenn never talks to me. I barely even knew Glenn existed. And now, he's offering me half a sandwich?!

And giving me a compliment, too?

. . . That's it: They feel *sorry* for me. This is like someone's last meal before walking the plank. The thought of the Doomsday Geeks, the absolute *un-coolest* kids in school feeling *sorry* for me makes everything seem much worse. My heart, which has been pounding hard since the notebook went missing, begins thumping like the loud bass in a sports car.

And don't get me started on Samantha. Her questions and suspicious expression tell me all I need to know. The gossip has already spread about everything I've written down . . . and there may have been some hearts around her name on some of the pages. The thought of her *knowing* is—for once, I can't find the right word. Usually I can, but not today. My little cage full of words is now empty, replaced by my rapidly beating heart. That's it. This is officially the *worst* day. Possibly, of all time.

"Last chance for half a sandwich!" Glenn says, waggling his cheddar on wheat in front of my face.

"No! I mean . . . no thanks, Glenn. I—I already ate."

With that, I turn around and walk away, deciding not to go through the lunch line after all. In an emergency, Saramus Dent would say, you don't need food.

THINGS JUST GET WORSE IN MATH CLASS. MRS. PRUGGLE CALLS on me before I've even gotten out my book or pencil.

"Damien Seeley."

"Yes?"

"There's something different about you today."

"There . . . there is?"

"Yes, indeed." Mrs. Pruggle has a cuddly name, but she's not cuddly at all. She's tall, with sharp elbows and hair that pokes out every which way. If she's explaining an especially hard math problem, she usually plays with the spikes in her hair. She'll tuck one behind her ear and another one will spring up and she'll have to do it all over again. Right now, I can't help but picture all of that spiky hair as rows and rows of teeth.

"Yes, I'm trying to put my finger on it." As she says this, Mrs. Pruggle strolls up and down the aisles of the classroom. Every three desks or so, she stops to drum her fingertips over the desktop. The other kids shift in their seats. Mrs. Pruggle scares everybody. Not just because she's the hardest grader of any teacher, but also because of something else. I think it's because she makes you feel like she can see through you. Which pretty much explains how I'm feeling at this exact second.

"Oh, I've got it!" she suddenly says, stopping in her tracks. She points at me with a long, pale finger. "You're with us today. You're *present*."

What does she mean? I can't help but feel a little annoyed. I mean, it's not like I've ever missed class.

"You're present, and you're not *doodling* through my whole class today. You don't have your notebook with you." I feel the other kids staring at me. If they didn't know about the missing notebook before, they definitely do now. I feel a Fire Blush begin to heat the base of my neck. I'm pretty sure this is going to be a bad blush.

"Oh, sorry," I say, like an idiot. "I left it at home?"

"You're asking me that like it's a question," Mrs.

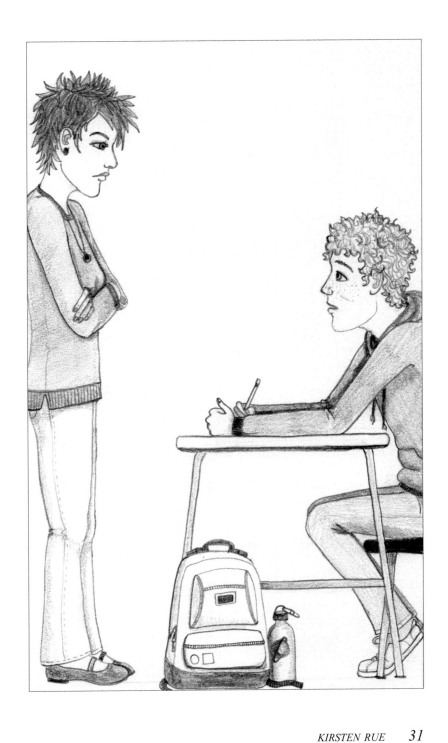

Pruggle says coolly, crossing her arms over her chest. "But the truth is, I'm glad to have your full attention today." My Fire Blush is going strong now. I'm sure my face looks as red as one of the limp tomatoes Halsey School serves with its "salads."

"Now," she says, walking back to the whiteboard. "Let's start solving for x, okay?"

I'm just glad to open my book and put my nose in it as far as it will go. At least this way, no one will be able to see my bright red face anymore. I'm not sure why Mrs. Pruggle decided that today was Make Damien Miserable in Front of Everyone Day. I know I'm not the best in math, but I'm not the worst. I never crack jokes in class or shout out the wrong answer. I just sit there, listening as much as I have to. With the rest of my brain, I usually add to Saramus Dent's story. Sometimes I draw a maze along the edge of a notebook page. Anything to make the class go faster. I guess Mrs. Pruggle noticed.

As Mrs. Pruggle blabs on and on about equations, I can feel my blush finally start to fade. I take out a sheet of plain printer paper from home. I begin to make a list.

Suspects
1. Glenn (Why else would he act so nice?)
2. Samantha Cho ☹
3. Ms. Arple (She was staring at me pretty hard today.)
4. A stranger
5. Mrs. Pruggle?

I scratch my head, trying to think of another name to add to the list. Just then, I feel a soft tap on the back of my right shoulder. A small, crumpled piece of paper drops onto the desk. I unwrap it. Written in small capital letters, it says, WHO TOOK YOUR NOTEBOOK?

I've read enough mystery books to know a ransom note when I see one. I don't recognize the handwriting, though, and I'm too afraid to turn around. Mrs. Pruggle is looking over towards me again. She must have heard the rustling paper. *Man, I hate this class.* I know it can't be the guy who always sits behind me. He wouldn't care. Someone passed it to him, and he passed it to me. As slowly as I can, I take the note off the desk and stuff it in my jeans.

When the bell finally rings, I stand up as fast as I can to look around. Everyone has their heads down and no one looks in my direction. Whoever passed the note is playing it cool. Nobody acts guilty. I'm so lost in thought looking around that I almost don't realize Mrs. Pruggle is calling my name for the second time that day.

"Damien Seeley!" she says, almost yelling.

"What?"

She crosses her arms again, and one of her spikes of hair tilts to one side. "Sometimes losing one of our shields is the best thing that can happen to us," she says.

Shield? I think, racing over today's lesson in my head. *Was there something in the equation called a shield?*

But with that, she just pats my arm. The next moment, she's cleaning off the whiteboard. It's like she doesn't even know I'm there. Of course, now the class is completely cleared out. There's no way to be a detective and get to the bottom of the note. I head to my next class, my heart nervously thumping again.

Out there is my notebook, and somewhere out there, someone is reading it.

———————

LATER THAT DAY WHEN I'M HOME FROM SCHOOL, I SIT IN THE TV room with Hildy instead of going upstairs to my room. I don't feel much like writing anyway. It doesn't feel right, somehow, without the notebook. It's almost like I'm missing the part of my hand that helps me to curve my fingers around a pencil. Saramus Dent will have to wait.

Hildy is surprised when I sit down on the chair across from her. She's watching her regular show about a group of people that rescue dogs. There are always sirens going off and lots of close-ups of dog snouts. Whenever a new dog comes on screen, Hildy sighs, "Oh, that one. That one is my dog. I love that dog." She knows there's NO WAY Mom and Dad will let us have a dog.

"I believe in responsibility," Mom always says. Hildy and I know that's just a cop-out. Mom is always repeating smart-sounding words from her job as a school psychologist. Mostly, they translate to mean, "That is not going to happen."

"Since when do you like my show?" Hildy asks, crunching on a Cheetoh. Cheetohs are another thing we are definitely not allowed to have.

"I like dogs."

"No, you don't. You don't like anything I like. Because it's not *dramatic* enough for you." Even though this is her favorite show, Hildy is also playing with her phone during commercials. Her attention is always bouncing this way and that. It bounces almost as much as her hair. "Look at this," she laughs, shoving her phone in my face. "Look at what my friend just texted me."

"R U there?" the text says, "i think the first dog looks like mr. diavolo." Hildy chuckles at the joke.

"Your friend spelled 'their' wrong," I say.

"Gosh, Damien, do you have *no* sense of humor?"

"I do. But I'm just saying. It should be T-H-E-R-E."

Hildy rolls her eyes at me and throws herself back against the couch. "I give up!" she says loudly. "Damien, you have killed me with your nerdiness." Her eyes squint as she looks at me. "No, but seriously. Shouldn't you be, like, *writing* or something?"

When I think of everything that's happened today—the missing notebook, the mysterious ransom note, Mrs. Pruggle, the Doomsday Geeks—my head starts to spin.

"I lost it," I lie.

"Well, Dad'll be mad. He's the one who bought it," Hildy says. "I just hope you didn't put anything *embarrassing* in there."

"Like what?"

"Like love notes to a *certain someone*." Oh, great. This again.

"Hildy," I say, in the coldest voice I can muster. "You are the dumbest person I know."

Just then, the commercial break ends and a close-up of a new dog comes on screen. This one is an orange color and has pointy ears like a little fox. "Awww, that's my dog," Hildy says in a quiet voice. She doesn't look at me. I think I might have actually hurt her feelings with that insult.

EVEN THAT NIGHT AT DINNERTIME, I'M NOT OFF THE HOOK about the missing notebook.

"How's your book coming along?" Mom asks. "What's new in the galaxy?" One time I was stupid enough to explain the world of Saramus Dent to Mom and Dad. Now, they always ask embarrassing questions about the "galaxy."

"It's fine," I lie again. I glance over at Hildy to see if she's going to spill the beans. Normally, that's basically her favorite thing to do, but she's just quietly cutting her piece of chicken in half. She doesn't look at me.

BEFORE BED, I PULL OUT MY LIST OF SUSPECTS ONE LAST time and add this to the bottom of it: 6. Anyone in Mrs. Pruggle's fifth period math class.

HALSEY MIDDLE SCHOOL

6

Troubles in the Galaxy

Saramus Dent's headache had started to clear. He had just received a spacegram from his commander across the galaxy. He opened it with his blasto-gun. Green ink glowed against the sky. "Dent, we need you on that planet," the spacegram said. "If you're low on oxygen, find one of the oxygen banks hidden in the red rocks. But don't abandon the galaxy, Dent. Whatever you do."

Dent waited for the glowing ink to fade. Then, he stood up and groaned. Just when he got ready to ditch this weirdo galaxy once and for all, a spacegram had to come. Still, he had to admit that his commander was right. He couldn't just leave.

EVEN THOUGH I ALMOST MAKE UP A FAKE COUGH AND headache the next morning, in the end I still go to school. I just hate breaking the rules. I think I'm probably the only kid at Halsey School who's such a goody-goody. I've definitely seen Hildy run some Kleenex under the bathroom faucet before. Then, she'll turn on her best sad face and exclaim, "Ew, Dad, look! My nose is *dripping!*"

My body feels the same as yesterday. Jumpy. Sweaty. I scan the faces of everyone in my homeroom class and between class periods. Is anyone looking at me funny? Is that a new thing, or did people *always* look at me funny? After second period, I pass Samantha Cho in the hall. I try to look away, pretend like I'm waiting to get a drink at the drinking fountain. She looks straight at me, her glossy black hair swinging against her cheeks. Her lips move as if she's about to say my name. She's forming a "D," I just know it! I don't wait to find out, though. Instead, I dive towards the water fountain. The water sprays all over my nose while Samantha swishes past behind me. I pretend to drink water until finally an eighth grader I don't know taps on my back.

"Um, dude. Turn's up."

BACK AT MY LOCKER BEFORE FOURTH PERIOD, I LOOK IN just to make sure that the notebook hasn't magically appeared. It hasn't. However, something else has: another note! It floats down from where my mystery notebook stealer must have shoved it through the locker door. I look around, but no one else has noticed. I snatch it up and unfold it.

YOU SHOULDN'T IgNORE ME. ARE YOU OK?

Now this is confusing. A threat that I shouldn't ignore this mystery person . . . mixed with a question about me being okay? *No, I'm not okay. I'm freaked out!* Who is this person? I have practically no friends at Halsey or anyone that I talk to, and yet somehow this *certain person* (I think of Hildy's words) knows me—and where my locker is, too. The whole thing is too weird. What do they want? Maybe it's like the mystery books I've read. Someone wants me to hand off a briefcase full of money in exchange for the notebook. Well, at least five bucks or something. I wish I'd emptied out my piggy bank before school this morning.

I almost decide not to eat lunch at all today—it seems too risky after everything that's been going on. Turns out I don't get much of a choice, though. Before I can stop him, Glenn appears out of nowhere, grabs my arm, and starts pulling me towards the lunchroom.

"Hey man! What's up?" he says. He smiles at me and pushes his glasses up on his nose with his other hand. I flinch. I can't help it. Glenn doesn't seem to notice, or if he does, he doesn't say anything. "I was hoping you'd sit with us today," he says. "We have something we want to ask you." I try to wiggle my arm out from his grip, but Glenn is surprisingly strong for one of the Doomsday Geeks. In fact, I realize I've never really *looked* at Glenn before. I kinda thought of all the Geeks as one big unit with glasses and weird haircuts and the wrong jeans. I knew not that much separated me from them, but I wanted to be sure to keep whatever *did* separate me very clear.

For a moment, I think of how I would always make a big sigh whenever I sat down at their table. The message of that sigh was clear, and I always meant for the other nearby tables to hear it, too. That sigh was supposed to say, "I am not one of these Geeks and I'm only sitting with them against my will." Now, looking at Glenn, I think that he actually looks different from the other guys. Actually, all the guys look different. One has red hair. One has skin the color of caramel. Yes, Glenn's jeans are a little *weird* but it's not like he's covered in purple spots or anything. Too bad I didn't think through all of this sooner, before the Geeks must have found my notebook. That's why they're targeting me now, right?

I search back through my memories. Did I write anything about them in there? I can't remember, but if

I did, you can bet it was something mean. Glenn steers me to the Doomsday Table, and all the other guys look up from the laptop screen they're gazing at. A carton of chocolate milk sits dangerously close to the keyboard. Right in the center of the group, smack dab in front of the computer, sits Samantha. My stomach lurches. It feels like someone is kicking me from the inside. So. This is it. The Geeks found my notebook. It was probably Glenn that pushed the note into my locker just before coming to find me. I did ignore him yesterday. Kinda. They've probably uploaded every page of my notebook onto that laptop. I mean, isn't that the kind of stuff they do? And Samantha Cho is their ringleader . . . which can only mean . . . she *knows*.

With a surge of superhuman—almost Saramus Dent-like strength—I rip my arm from Glenn's grip. Glenn and the whole table of Geeks stare at me. "Um, I'm feeling kinda sick," I mumble. Then, I book it out of the lunchroom. I mean, like, I really *run*. If I wanted to avoid the other sixth graders watching me, this is for sure not the best way to do it. Stella Sweet pauses to stare as I race past her, her stick of pink gum frozen mid-chew in her mouth.

"Mr. Seeley!" Ms. Arple yells sharply. "No running!"

I'm not listening, though. I sprint out of the lunchroom, banging the doors behind me. I don't stop until I've reached the library. Two other sixth graders—Tina and Julian, I think—look up and glare at me as I crash through, breathing hard.

When my breathing has finally slowed down, it hits me. *That was the dumbest thing I've ever done.* I mean, seriously, what WAS that? As if I could just run away from all of my problems. The notebook is gone, and so are the parts of my world that were documented there. It feels sad. Like all your closest friends moving away at once. Not that I would even know what having friends feels like. I just sprinted away from the only people who have ever invited me to eat lunch in Halsey School. I probably hurt Glenn's hand, too. I keep picturing Samantha's face: how her forehead wrinkled as I made my stupid excuse. She almost looked hurt. I think of her this morning—how she was about to talk to me, but I rushed away. This whole year, I kept writing in my notebook, complaining about being alone. Maybe that wasn't all Halsey School's fault. Or the Geeks' fault. And definitely not Samantha's fault.

A Fire Blush starts to burn through the skin of my face. This time, I'm not even sure it'll go away.

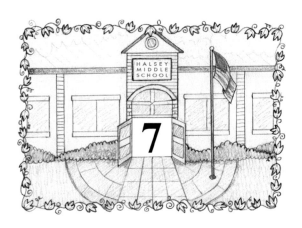

HALSEY
MIDDLE
SCHOOL

7

The Thief

"Ah ha! I found you!" Dent was back in action. Someone had to save the Galaxy from the Hildebeast. The beast was even smellier than usual, its back covered with different tufts of neon hair. Still, as Dent got closer, he realized something was wrong with the Hildebeast. It sat on the green dirt of the planet making a sound like someone hitting all the keys on a piano at the same time. Could it be? Dent could barely believe his eyes. The Hildebeast was wounded.

As I open the front door after school, my backpack feels weighed down with all the things that have happened in the last few days. All I want to do is go to my room, pull my favorite science fiction book off the shelf, and read it until I fall asleep. I sense something is off, though, as I step inside and start hanging up my coat on one of the pegs. Somebody is crying and sniffling. Since my parents aren't home from work yet, it's not very hard to figure out whom. It's Hildy.

At first, I decide I'll just ignore her and go straight upstairs. I take off my shoes super quietly and start creeping across the carpet. She doesn't have her rescue dog show playing, which is unusual.

"Damien?" Hildy calls from the living room. I can practically hear the snot in her voice. *Caught!*

"Yes . . ." I reply, sighing. I guess I'm going to have to go in there now, and like, pat her on the back or something. I think I'd rather deal with the Hildebeast than a crying, real-life Hildy.

"Damien. I can hear you!" Hildy wails. "You have to come in here."

Could this day be any more insane?

I trudge into the living room. "What is it?" Hildy is watching her show, but it's on mute. The camera is moving over a row of dogs' faces. They look almost as sad as her. She sits, surrounded by wadded-up tissues. Her nose is red and leaky, and her eyes are all squinched up. Her chin is resting on her knees, and she's already changed into pajamas. Like everything Hildy owns, her pajamas are covered in a dog print. Bursting into a huge sob, Hildy reaches behind her back and slams a notebook down onto the floor in front of her.

I stare at it. It has a soft leather cover and the initials D.O.S. burned onto the front. I blink a couple of times. I almost can't believe it. There it is. My notebook.

"I'm sorry!" Hildy sobs, releasing a fresh wave of tears. "Mom's mad at me. She told me I had to apologize to you. ALONE. But I'm sorry, okay?"

That does sound like something my mom would say.

I can picture her now: "Hildy, it's time to take some proper responsibility for what you've done."

For now, I'm so shocked that I can't even be mad. I carefully pick up the notebook and flip it open. There they are: the Saramus Dent adventures and all my other scribbles. Every page is still there, even my notes about Samantha Cho. A feeling of relief washes over me and I hold the notebook very, very tightly to my chest. That's where I always hold it: right over my heart.

As she watches me cradle the notebook, Hildy rolls her eyes through her tears. "Like I could even read it, anyway! Half of the words seemed made up, and the rest were so messy, I could barely tell a 'p' from a 'g'!"

Hildy seems so upset that I don't want to yell at her. Plus, the energy I would've used to punch her in the arm has been taken up by my dash from the lunchroom earlier today. She keeps sniffling. I can tell that she's feeling sorry for herself. Hildy hates it when people yell at her. She hates being wrong and having to say, "I'm sorry." So, actually, this is kind of a big day for her.

"Why . . . why did you take it?"

She shoots me a scowl, her eyes almost swollen shut with tears. "Because at first I wanted to see what you wrote about me! I took it from your bag when you left it in the backseat. On the way to school." *So, that's why it had been in my backpack in the morning, but gone by the time I went to my locker!*

"And also, I wanted to get back at you, okay?" Her voice is small and mouselike.

"But for what? What did I ever do to you?" A little flicker of anger finally flares up.

"Do you ever think how *I* feel? Like, oh, here's perfect Damien. He's so *responsible* and so *smart* and look at his *amazing* imagination. How do you think it feels to be the stupid one? I mean, just last night, you called me 'the stupidest person in the world.'"

"But I didn't mean that."

"Sure, sure. But everyone knows I'm going to have to like, *re-take* English, and meanwhile, you're just dreaming away upstairs. And Mom and Dad let you off completely off the hook."

I have to admit, she has a point. Mom and Dad tend to let me skip out on chores as long as I keep getting A's. All I have to say is, "I need to go work on my writing," and they nod and smile. No questions asked.

"I guess I just wanted to get back at you," Hildy repeats. "But then Mom found the notebook in my room and figured it all out. And told me I was being very *hurtful*." "Hurtful" is another favorite word of Mom's. Maybe her second favorite after "responsible." "She said I had to apologize to you and talk things through. Even though she knows I hate that!" A couple more tears trickle down Hildy's cheeks.

I don't know what it is. Maybe seeing Hildy break down like this, or maybe just the relief of knowing my notebook is safe makes any anger seem pointless. I mean, I have to live in the same house with Hildy, after all. That's at least five more years of my life. "Well," I say, "I'm sorry I called you stupid. I don't think that. You're not."

Hildy nods. Her chin wobbles. "Oh," she adds, "and I'm sorry about making up that whole crush or whatever." She waves her hand in the air.

"What crush? You mean, about a *certain someone*?"

"Yeah, it was dumb, right? I knew you wouldn't fall for it. But, still. I'm sorry. I made it up."

"So . . . there is no *certain someone*?"

"Nah." Hildy shrugs. I guess I should be glad. This means that Samantha never knew I have feelings for her. Until today, when I ran away without speaking, we really *had* been friends. And only friends. Weirdly, now that I know that Samantha and I are only friends, I almost feel disappointed. There had been a little excitement, buried deep inside, that maybe she knew. And that perhaps her knowing might lead to . . . well, I guess anything would be better than me running away from her table and avoiding her in the halls.

Hildy has finally stopped crying. She's hiccupping and wiping the rest of her tears with a snotty tissue.

"Can I un-mute my show now? It's almost over."

"Sure," I say. The camera is now just focused on one dog—a black and white fluffy one with a patch of brown over his eye.

"Look at that dog, Hildy," I say. "That's my dog."

She smiles. "Let's name him Billy Jo."

As I walk in through Halsey's doors the next day—Friday—I know I have things to face. I have to apologize to the Doomsday Geeks. And Glenn. I have to figure out who was passing me notes. And I have to say something . . . *anything* . . . to Samantha Cho. In homeroom, I take out the little sheet of paper where I was keeping track of my suspects. Now, I know who stole the notebook—Hildy—so this time I'm only thinking about the identity of the mysterious note leaver. I cross out every name. Except one, that is. Only one person had really seen me with that notebook, and would know it was important to me, besides Hildy. Only one person could honestly write YOU SHOULDN'T IgNORE ME. There was only one person I'd been avoiding. I look at my new list:

Suspects

1. ~~Glenn (Why else would he act so nice?)~~
2. ~~Samantha Cho~~ ☹
3. ~~Ms. Arple (She was staring at me pretty hard today.)~~
4. ~~A stranger~~
5. ~~Mrs. Pruggle?~~
6. ~~Anyone in Mrs. Pruggle's fifth period math class~~

I know, finally, what I need to do. I rip a page out of my newly-found notebook.

Dear Samantha,

Meet me by the old tetherball pole at recess. Sorry I've been weird.

- Damien

It's probably not the most moving note I've ever written, but it'll have to do. On my way to math class, I stop by Samantha's locker and *Swish!*, the note slips inside the door. No backing out now.

DURING MATH, I NOTICE MRS. PRUGGLE STARING AT ME again. I see her eyes narrow as she notices that my notebook is back.

"I hope I still have your full attention, Damien Seeley." She's writing a long equation on the board in a string of x's and y's, and has paused mid-x.

"Yeah. I'm listening." She nods, satisfies, and turns back to the board. I slip the notebook back into my pack. No need to be drawing *that* kind of attention from the scariest teacher at Halsey School.

DURING RECESS, MY HEART IS RACING AGAIN. I KEEP TRYING to compose what I'll say to Samantha when . . . *if* . . . she comes outside. I try to use all my best words and put them together in a nice, flowing speech in my brain. I picture them all like one of the commander's spacegrams: rows of glowing green words. I rearrange them; try out new combinations. "Dearest Samantha . . . Samantha, I've always thought there was something special about you . . ." I want to sound like Saramus Dent. Or someone from one of my books. But I have a sinking feeling that I'll only be sounding like Damien Seeley, squeaky voice, thin arms, and all.

I'm so lost in my mental spacegram that I almost miss Samantha coming my way. She picks her way lightly over the frosty pavement. She's wearing a pink, puffy coat that goes down almost to her knees. On one arm, she's stuck a pin with a peace sign on it. She must be switching things up. Usually she only likes math symbols. Samantha has always been direct. She walks straight up to me, her cheeks reddened from the fall air.

"So. You wanted to talk to me?" My mental spacegram vaporizes, just like I knew it would. I'll have to wing this one.

"Yeah. Um, I'm sorry that I ignored you. I know it

was you. You were the one who sent me those notes. In Mrs. Pruggle's math class and in my locker. I didn't even think it could be . . . I mean, you're in advanced math, not Mrs. Pruggle's class . . ."

Samantha interrupts me, holding up one of her small hands. "Correction," she says. "I'm not in your class but I asked Glenn to pass it to you. He's in that class."

"Glenn?!"

"Yeah, he passed it to someone that passed it to you. Though he said you never talk to him."

"I didn't even know he was in my class! I thought all of you were in advanced math. I never even noticed Glenn before." And that's the truth. Had he really been there the whole time? For all those weeks!? I have to admit to myself that I've been a total jerk. I never even said "hi" to Glenn or paid attention to him when he must have answered one of Mrs. Pruggle's questions.

Samantha shakes her head impatiently. "Look. Why are we talking about math? Yes, I did pass you both notes." Samantha looks down, rubbing at a pebble on

the pavement with the toe of her shoe. "I was worried about you. I saw you looking all stressed out that day, and I just *knew* you had lost something. And I thought, what's the one thing Damien wouldn't want to lose? It was pretty easy to figure out. I wasn't trying to scare you with my notes, honest. I thought you would know it was me! It seems like you never talk to any of us. Or to me. I mean, I know we're 'geeks,' but still . . . you've been acting different. So, since you wouldn't talk to me in person, I tried talking to you in writing."

"I know. I'm sorry, Samantha. I thought someone stole my notebook, but I was totally wrong. Of course. It was my *sister* who took it." I snort a little bit, remembering Hildy's tearful confession yesterday. "No one in sixth grade really even knew it was gone. Or cared. Except for you." I take a deep breath. This is the longest I've talked to Samantha in a very long time, and it seems to be going okay. I still can't figure out the look on her face, but I don't think it's bad. "I'm always in my own little world, I guess," I continue. "Always in my head imagining my stories and everything. But once I lost my notebook . . . I realized, um, that maybe that's not such a good thing." My face feels warm, though thankfully a full-on Fire Blush isn't happening yet.

"Maybe not," Samantha says, doing that shrug that she does. "But I like what you write. That's what we wanted to ask you yesterday, me and the other guys. At lunch. We were going to ask you to join the group."

"To do math?!" I can barely conceal my horror.

"No! Geez, Damien, *everyone* knows how much you hate math. No, it was to be our club secretary. We were going to show you the blog we made."

Suddenly, the laptop and the whole group of them sitting at the lunch table makes sense. So, *that's* what Glenn wanted to talk to me about. I had almost missed my shot at having friends who actually wanted me around—who thought I *knew* something. I had missed the point like an asteroid whizzing miles away from Earth.

"I was sure someone stole it! Can you believe that? My notebook, I mean. I thought everyone was out to get me. And that even *Mrs. Pruggle* was in on it. I was, like, *delusional*."

"Wait," Samantha says, holding up her hand again. "What does 'delusional' mean? And what about Mrs. Pruggle?"

"It means I was making everything up in my own head! Mrs. Pruggle said something weird to me yesterday about being stronger without my shield. I don't know. That lady confuses me."

"Idiot," Samantha laughs. "She was talking about your notebook! She meant your notebook is your shield. And she meant, probably, that you've been using it as a shield to keep people out."

I blink, mouth open.

"Seriously, Damien, I thought English was your best subject."

For the first time in, I don't know, a *century*, I feel myself start to laugh. And the good news? Samantha is laughing, too.

―――――――

THE NEXT DAY AT LUNCH, I WALK STRAIGHT TO THE DOOMSDAY Geeks table.

"Hey, guys!" I say, waving.

From out of nowhere, I think of that phrase, "Fake it till you make it." Must be something my mom says. Well, today, I'm using it. I walk up to their table, smile, and take a seat. They scoot over, and from across the table, Glenn smiles.

"Mrs. Pruggle is intense, right?" he says.

"Yeah, she won't leave me alone!" I offer Glenn half of my sandwich.

"Yo," comes Samantha's breezy voice from behind me. "Scooch over, Damien."

Well played, dude, I think Dent would say. *Well played.*

Now, when Saramus Dent approached Cafetariana, he didn't feel like such an outsider. He was from that planet. Its smells and bizarre creatures didn't bother him so much anymore. Sure, the Green Forces were weird, but then, Dent was kind of weird himself. He had no birthday, never sneezed, and never had to use the bathroom. Definitely weird. After learning this, Dent was almost enjoying this time of general peace in the Globorz Galaxy.

Of course, he knew another adventure was only a blasto-shot away. . . .